BORIS
FOR THE WIN

by Andrew Joyner

BRANCHES
SCHOLASTIC INC.

Adventures are always just around the corner with BORIS!

Table of Contents

Introduction..................................... 1

Chapter One..................................... 9

Chapter Two 18

Chapter Three..................................25

Chapter Four 34

Chapter Five 41

Chapter Six 50

Chapter Seven..................................61

How to Make an Obstacle Course...73

Library of Congress Cataloging-in-Publication Data

Joyner, Andrew.
[Ready, set, Boris]
Boris for the win / Andrew Joyner.
p. cm. -- (Boris ; 3)
Originally published as Ready, set, Boris. Camberwell, Vic. : Puffin, c2011.
Summary: School field day is coming up and Boris and his friends are practicing hard because they are determined not to let Eddie win again, but on race day Boris is forced to choose between winning and friendship.
ISBN 978-0-545-48448-0 -- ISBN 978-0-545-48449-7 1. Warthog--Juvenile fiction. 2. Running races--Juvenile fiction. 3. Competition (Psychology)--Juvenile fiction. 4. Friendship--Juvenile fiction. 5. Schools--Juvenile fiction. [1. Warthog--Fiction. 2. Racing--Fiction. 3. Competition (Psychology)--Fiction. 4. Friendship--Fiction. 5. Schools--Fiction.] I. Title.
PZ7.J8573Bok 2013
823.92--dc23
2012046575

ISBN 978-0-545-48448-0 (hardcover) / ISBN 978-0-545-48449-7 (paperback)

12 11 10 9 8 7 6 5 4 3 2 1   13 14 15 16 17 18/0

Printed in China   38
First Scholastic printing, August 2013

Meet Boris.
He's a lot like you.

favorite
backpack

favorite
magnifying
glass

favorite
shirt

favorite book
(this week)

favorite
snack

favorite
yo-yo

He has lots of pets.

This is Frank.

This is a skink.

This is Tina.

This is Quince.

This is Lion.

This is Ethel.

Boris likes to walk to school with his friends.

This is Frederick.

This is their teacher.

This is Alice.

And he likes to dream.

Boris dreams of big leaps.

He dreams of big tricks.

And big treasure.

But mostly he dreams
about big adventures!

You'll never be bored when Boris is around!
So hitch a ride for his next adventure.
He could take you anywhere . . .
up in the clouds,
into a pyramid, or maybe
just around the corner.

CHAPTER ONE

Boris's class was practicing for Field Day.
There would be a high jump, a long
jump, an egg-and-spoon race, hurdles,
and a tug-of-war. But they were starting
with the round-the-track marathon.
Mrs. Huff led the class to the starting line.

Boris ran as fast as he could.

He wanted to win.

But he couldn't . . .

. . . quite . . .

. . . get there.

The problem was Eddie.

Eddie could run the fastest.

He could jump the highest.

And the longest.

When they tried the hurdles,
Eddie cleared them all with ease.

But Boris and Frederick
had some trouble.

CHAPTER TWO

After practice,
Boris, Frederick, and Alice
had lunch.

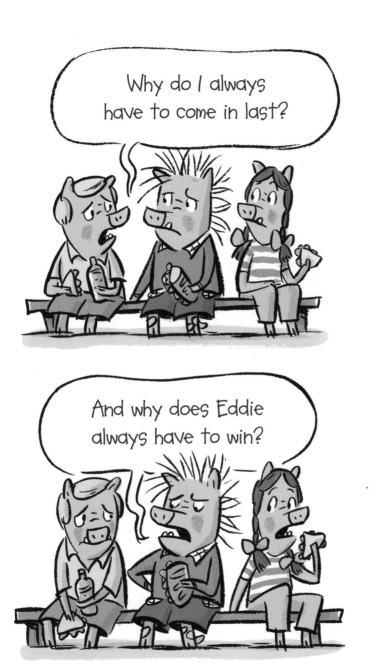

What they needed was a plan.

Boris thought.

And thought.

And thought.
Then he had an idea.

CHAPTER THREE

That afternoon, when Frederick
and Alice got to Boris's place . . .

. . . it looked a little different.

They trained every day after
school for the next week.

They did the high jump.

The long jump.

The tug-of-war.

The hurdles.

Even the egg-and-spoon race.

And finally, the night before
Field Day, they ran a marathon . . .

. . . all the way to
Frederick's house.

CHAPTER FOUR

It was Field Day.

Boris had never felt better,
and Alice was ready to go.

But Frederick didn't look so good.

He had the most terrible hay fever.

Boris got off to a great start.

He jumped his highest jump,

and cleared every hurdle.

But he still couldn't beat Eddie.

No one could beat Eddie.

Alice tried to cheer Boris up.

But Boris knew he'd have to try
even harder if he wanted to win.

CHAPTER FIVE

It was the most important
race of the day.

The round-the-track marathon.
Mrs. Huff waved the starting flag.

ACHOO!

They were off!

It was a long race,
so Boris took it easy at first.

Eddie was out front . . .

. . . but Boris was catching up.

Some of Eddie's friends
tried to slow Boris down.

But he
hurdled one.

He dodged
another.

And soon he was in second place.

Right behind Eddie.

They'd been running for a long time,
but Boris wasn't even tired.

They ran around the corner.
Boris could see the
finish line up ahead.

But suddenly he couldn't see Eddie.

I must be in front!

CHAPTER SIX

Boris turned his head.

Eddie was right behind him.

Then Boris noticed Frederick.
He wasn't even running.

He was barely walking.

Boris kept
running.

He was going to win!

But what about Frederick?

Boris ran back past Eddie,

back past Alice,

and back past the rest of his class.

Finally he reached Frederick.

CHAPTER SEVEN

Boris tried not to look
at the finish line.

He couldn't bear to watch Eddie win.
Not again.

But then Frederick noticed something
he knew Boris would want to see.

Look, Boris, look!

It was Alice!
She was
running faster
than she'd ever
run before.

She was in fourth place,

third place,

second place, and . . .

. . . across the finish line!

So Alice came in first.

Eddie came in second.

And Boris and Frederick?

Well,
they did win
something. . . .

THE END

MAKE YOUR OWN BACKYARD OBSTACLE COURSE BY BORIS

THINGS YOU NEED:

1. A stopwatch or an egg timer

2. Things from around your home to use as obstacles

3. Some friends or family to race with!

You can make an obstacle course using lots of things from around your home. Here are a few ideas.

HORSE TROT

Set up a row of buckets and race around them on your broom. Make sure you don't knock over any buckets!

Now turn the page....

JUNGLE LIMBO

Tie a rope between two trees and limbo under it. How low can you go? Don't forget to bend those knees!

TUNNEL FUN

Make a tunnel with a row of chairs. Then roll, kick, or crawl a ball through the tunnel.

HOSE HOP

Lay out a garden hose in a zigzag. Hop over it until you reach the end.

USE YOUR IMAGINATION! Grab your stopwatch and some friends and see who can make it around the course the fastest.

READY, SET, GO!

YOU'LL NEVER BE BORED WHEN BORIS IS AROUND! LOOK FOR HIS NEXT EXCITING ADVENTURE:

Boris is having a sleepover! He's camping in the backyard with Frederick and Alice. And they are not one bit scared of the dark. No way!

But what is that strange light moving around outside the tent? And what is making all of those strange, scary noises? It's up to Boris to find out. . . .

ANDREW JOYNER has never been good at sports. Although he did once captain his school Field Day team. All he had to do was lead the team in a march around the school track. Instead he marched straight into a fence. He was too busy waving to his mom and dad.